W9-AAZ-803

MARVEL

BLACK WIDOW™ JOINS THE MIGHTY AVENGERS™

Based on the Marvel comic book series
The Mighty Avengers
Adapted by Clarissa Wong
Illustrated by Mike Norton
and Hi-Fi Design

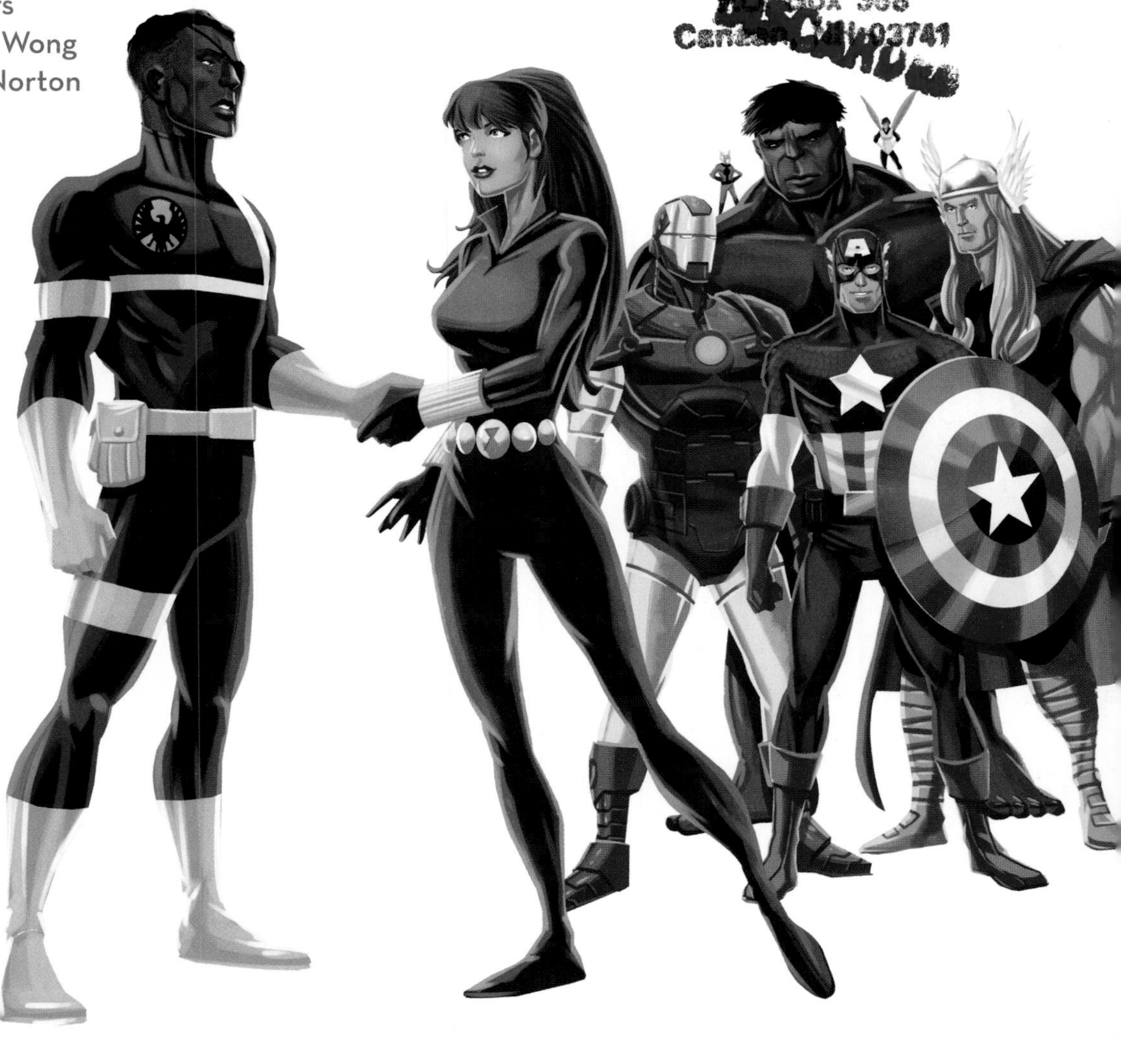

Published by Marvel Press, an imprint of Disney Book Group.

For information address Marvel Press, 114 Fifth Avenue, New York, New York 10011-5690.
Printed in the United States of America
First Edition
1 3 5 7 9 10 8 6 4 2
G658-7729-4-12074
ISBN 978-1-4231-4278-2

marvelkids.com

MARVEL
New York

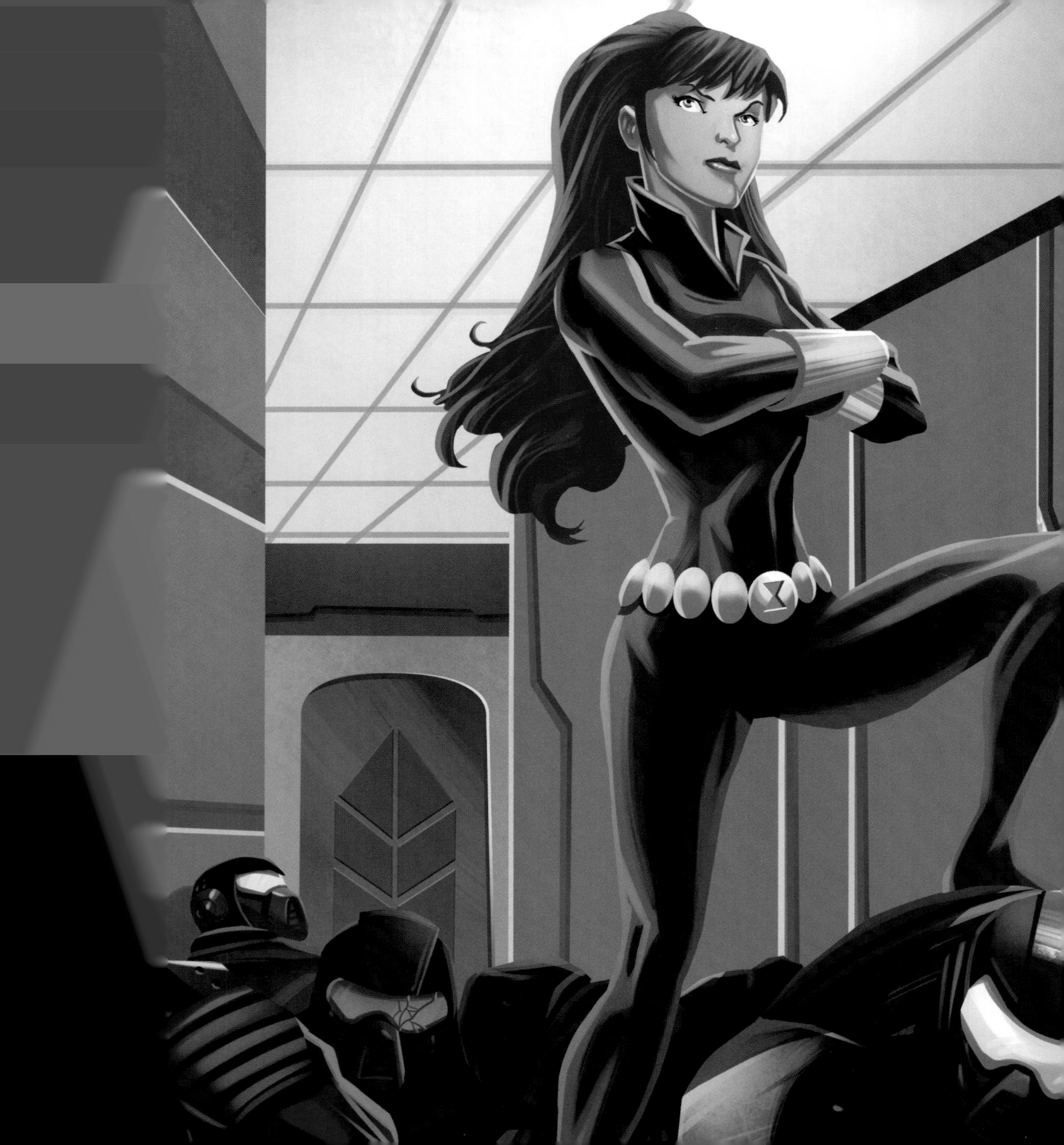

Natasha Romanova is the superspy **Black Widow.** But she wasn't always so tough. It took years of training. And she wasn't being tough for herself. She was doing it for her little brother, **Alexi.**

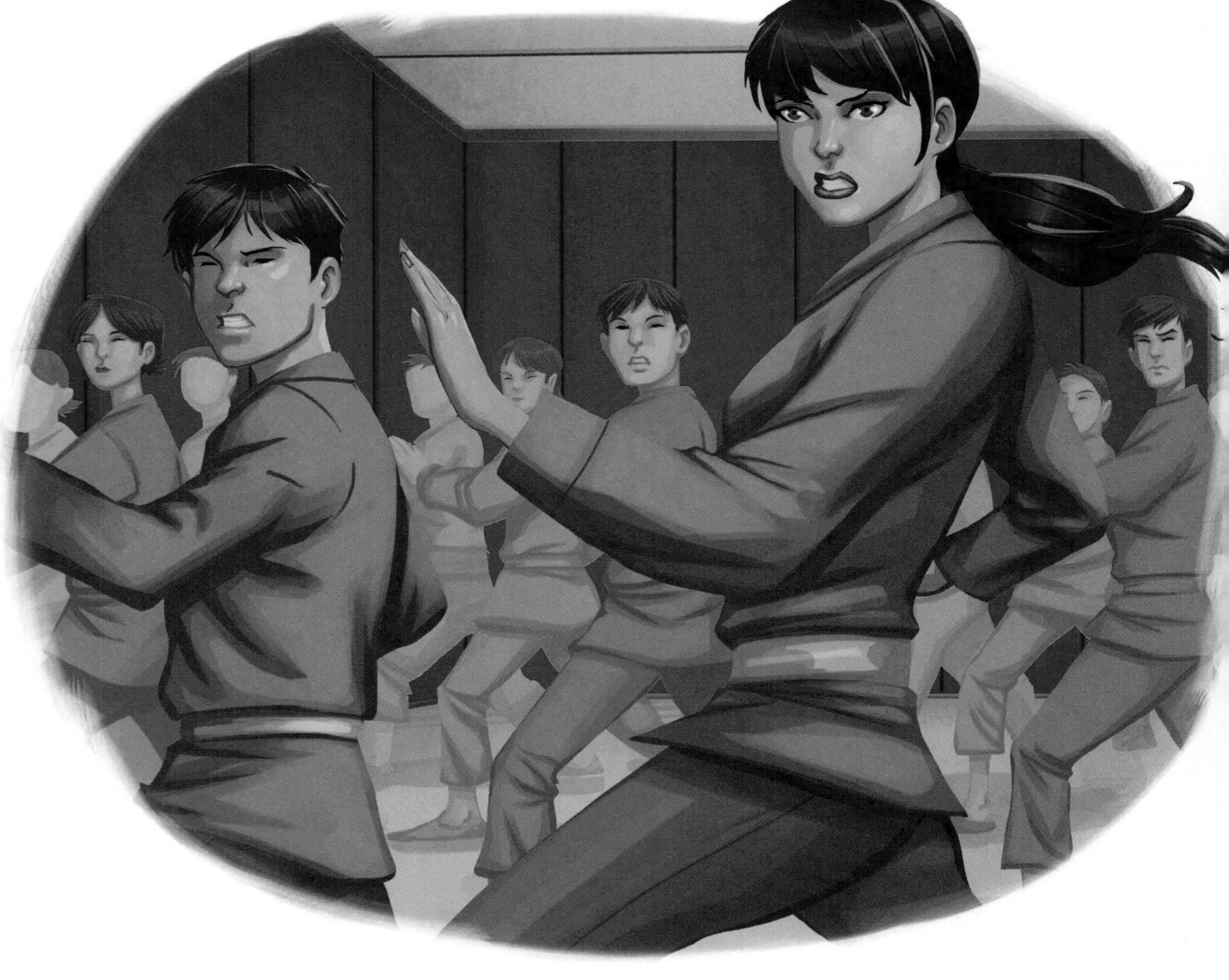

Natasha and Alexi grew up in an orphanage called **the Red Room.** But this orphanage was not like other orphanages. Natasha, Alexi, and the other children were trained to be **perfect spies.** They had to follow strict rules.

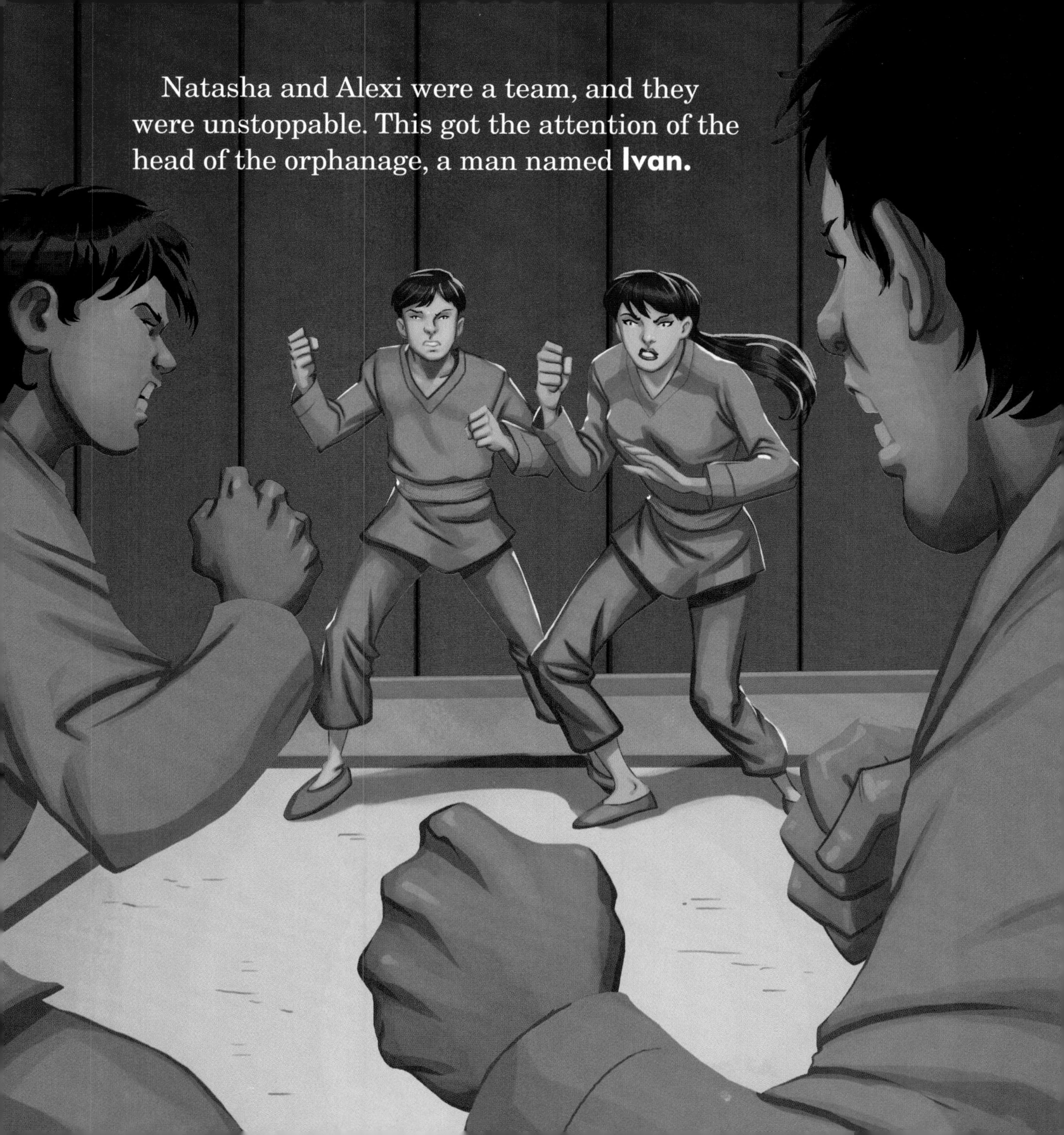

Natasha and Alexi were a team, and they were unstoppable. This got the attention of the head of the orphanage, a man named **Ivan.**

Ivan wanted Natasha to be his top spy. But that would mean leaving Alexi behind.

"I'll do it, but only if Alexi is my partner," Natasha said. **"We're family, and we always take care of each other."**

Ivan was surprised. No one ha ever made such a request before But he admired her toughness, and agreed.

As they got older, Alexi was worried he wasn't good enough.

"You're so good at this spy stuff, Natasha. **You're like a black widow.** I'm like a clumsy hippo, knocking into everything." Alexi shook his head with disappointment.

Natasha was worried. What would happen if she couldn't protect her brother?

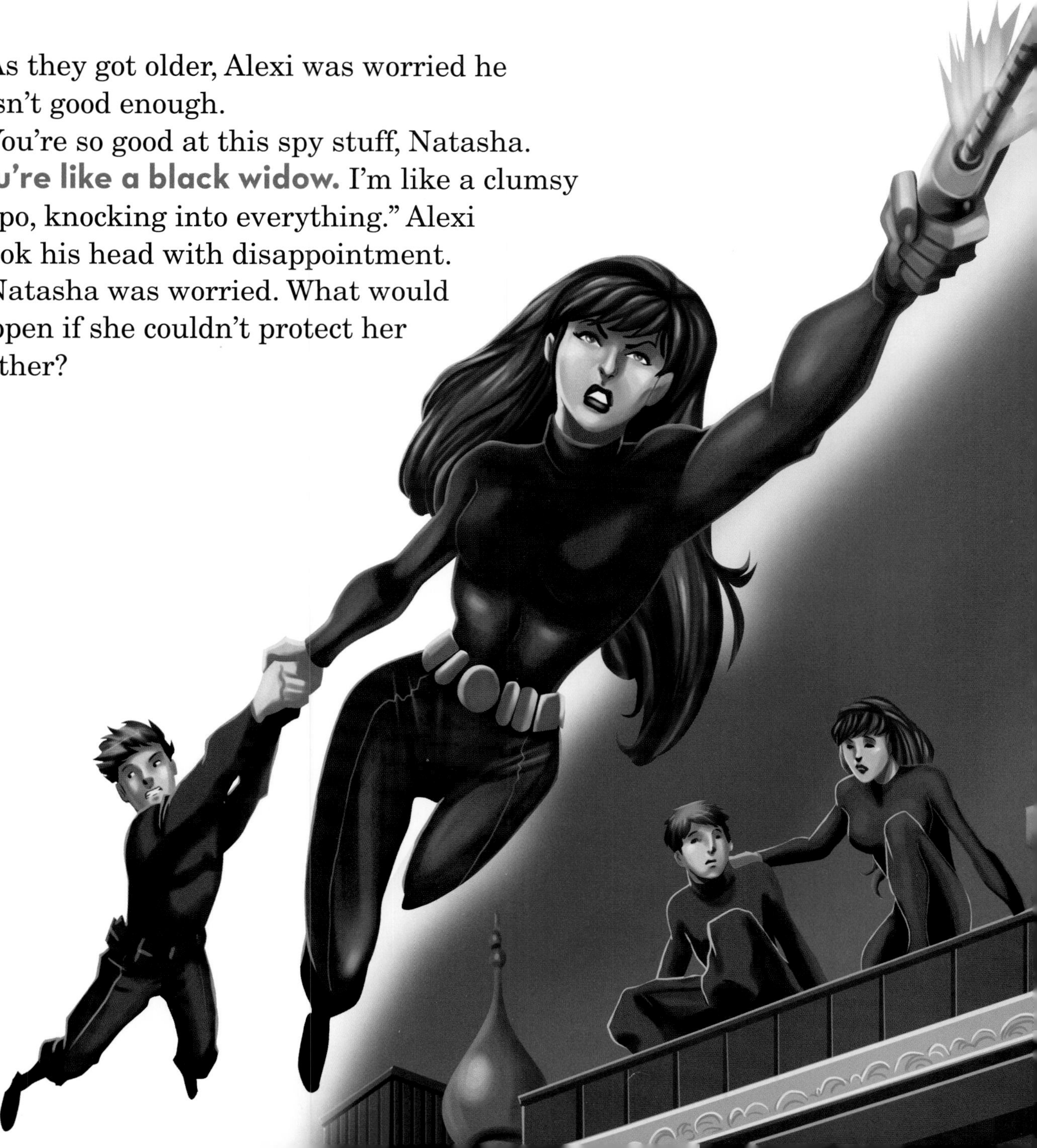

One day, Natasha was called into Ivan's office. "Alexi has failed too many missions. He knows too much. **We must erase his memory,**" Ivan said coldly.

If Alexi was brainwashed, he would not remember who Natasha was.

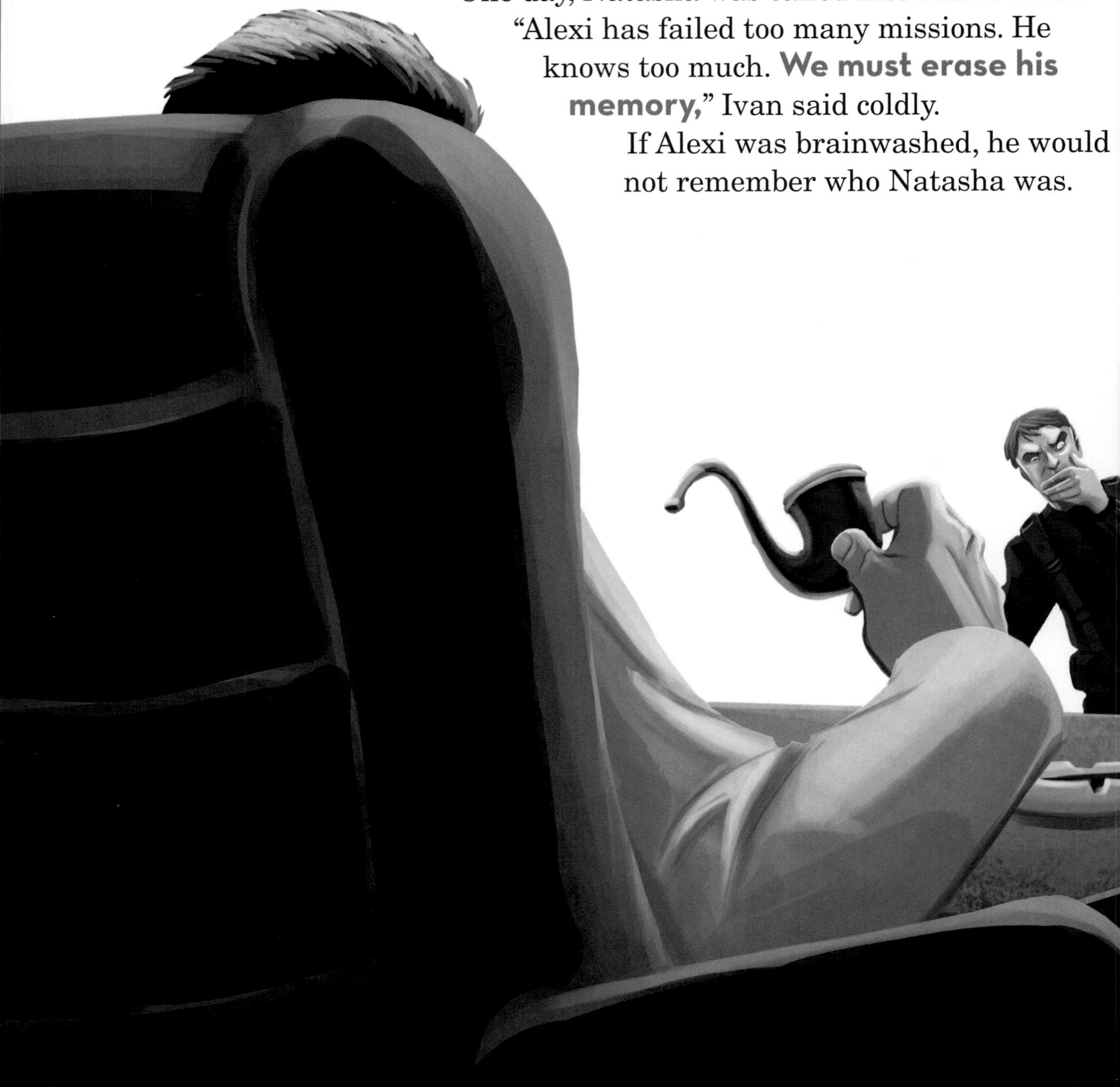

Natasha saw the evil in Ivan's eyes. "You can't. . ." she started to say. **She had to stand up for what was right.**

"The punishment for disobedience is to be expelled from the program, my dear!" Ivan declared. She fought back, but she was outnumbered.

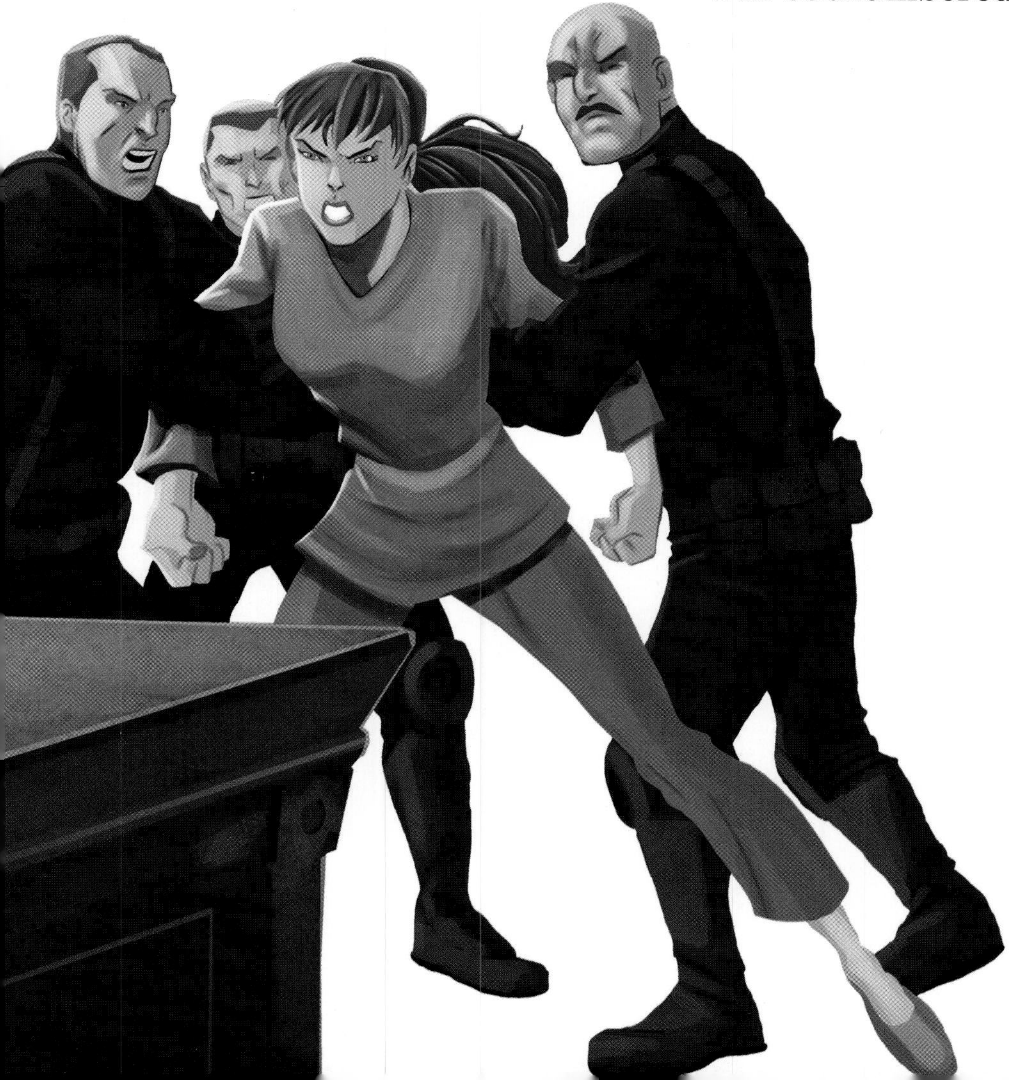

Ivan kept Alexi prisoner. But Natasha had an idea. She had heard of a team of Super Heroes called **the Avengers.** She would ask them for help.

Their leader's name was **Nick Fury,** and she would have to find a way into the **S.H.I.E.L.D.** headquarters to speak to him.

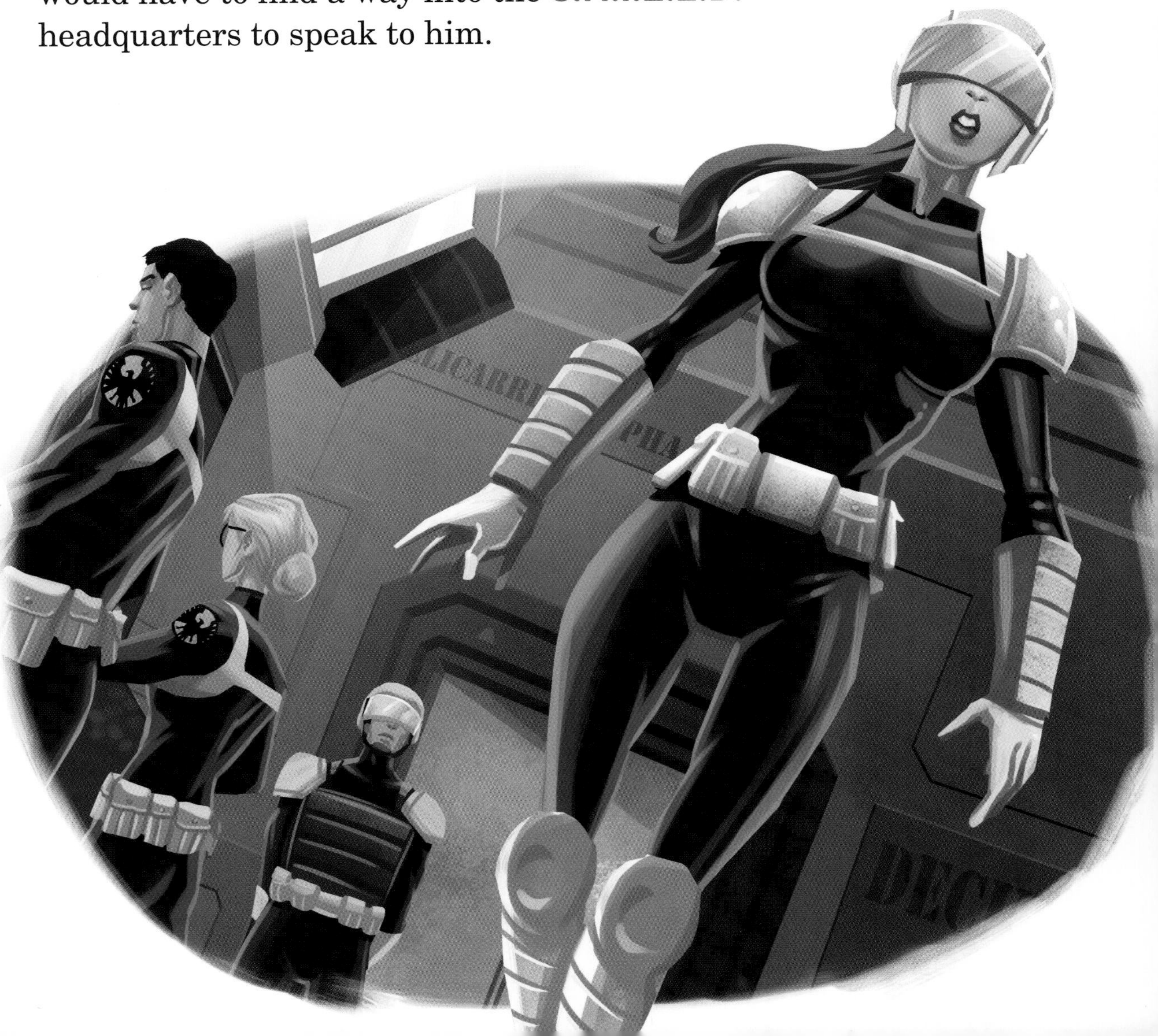

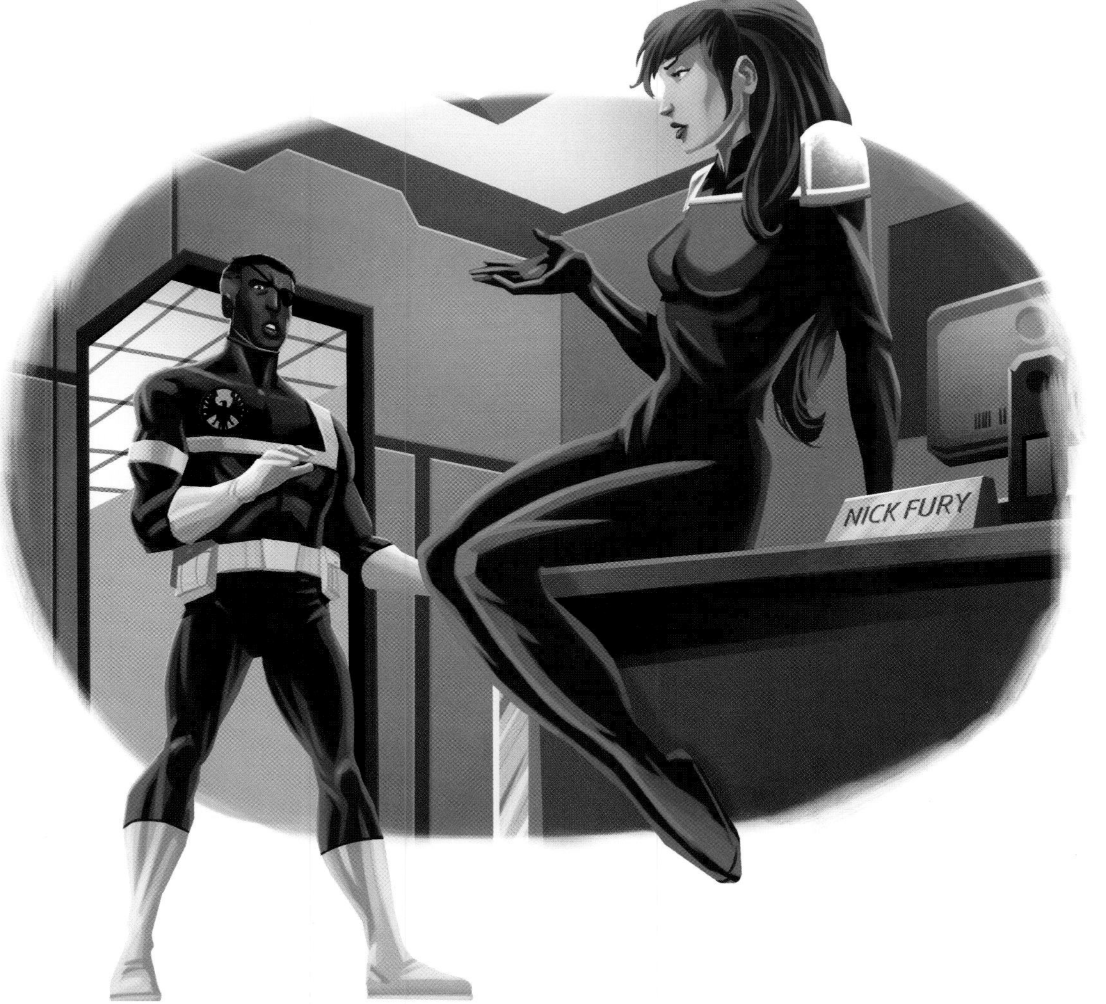
NICK FURY

Natasha was very good at being sneaky, and she soon made her way to Fury's office.

"I need your help, Mr. Fury," Natasha said.

"Well, you know who I am. But who are you?" Fury asked, raising an eyebrow.

"You can call me Natasha."

Natasha was surprised at how willing the Avengers were to help, even though none of them knew her.

"What Ivan is doing is wrong," **the Wasp** said.

The rest of the Avengers agreed.

"We have to rescue Alexi," **Captain America** said.

"But Natasha can't just go in without any way to defend herself. . ." **Tony Stark** said. **"I think I might have an idea."**

Natasha led the Avengers to the secret location of the Red Room. The Avengers freed the children. Natasha grinned. For the first time, completing a mission felt good.

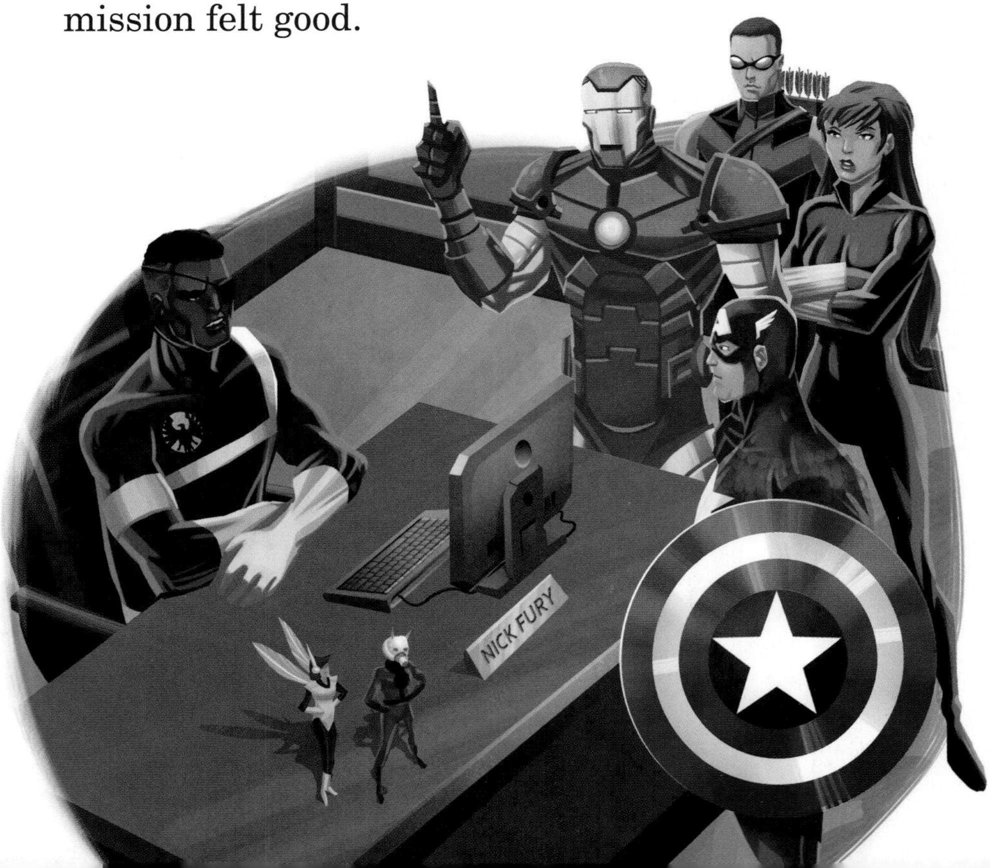
NICK FURY

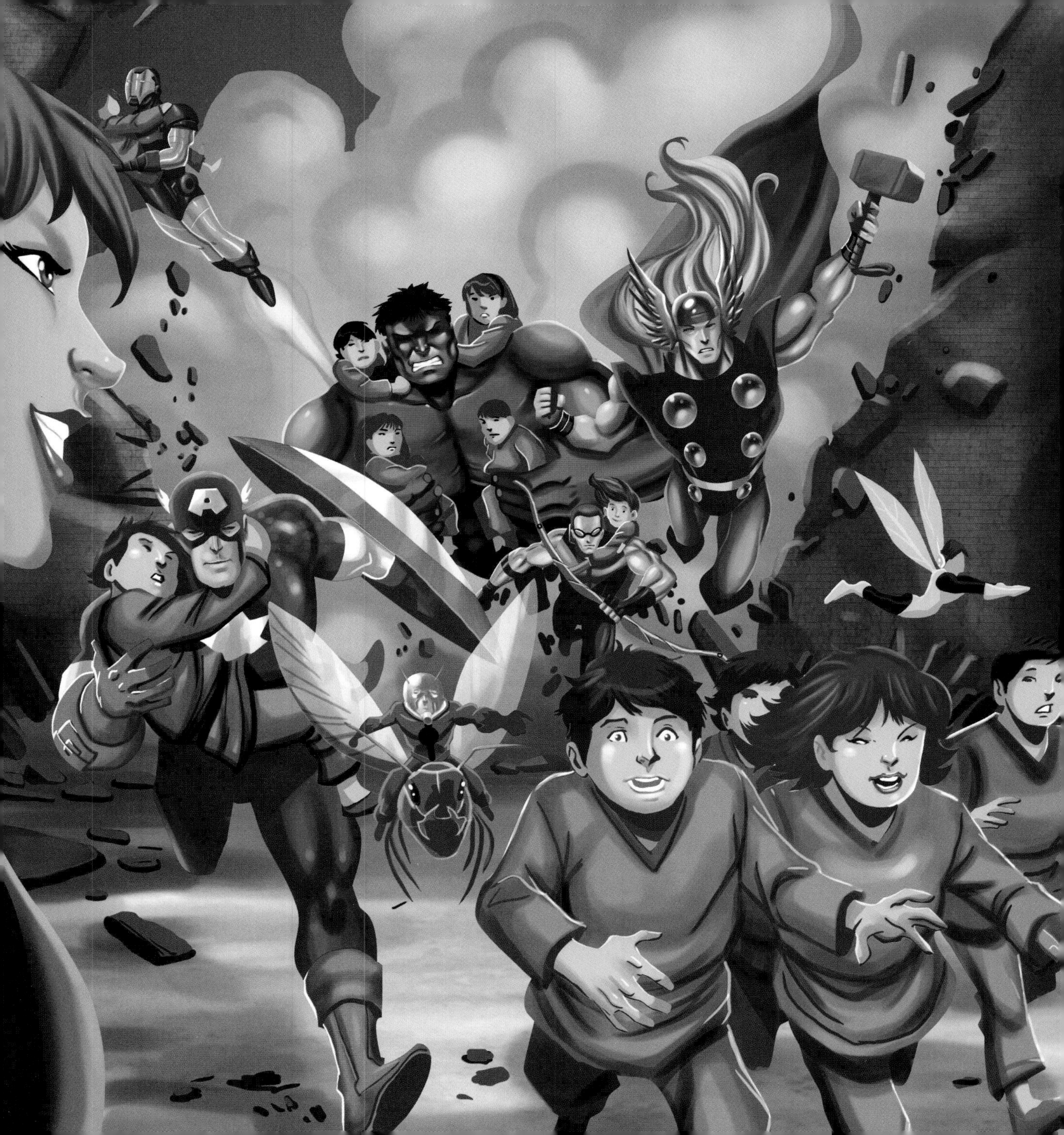

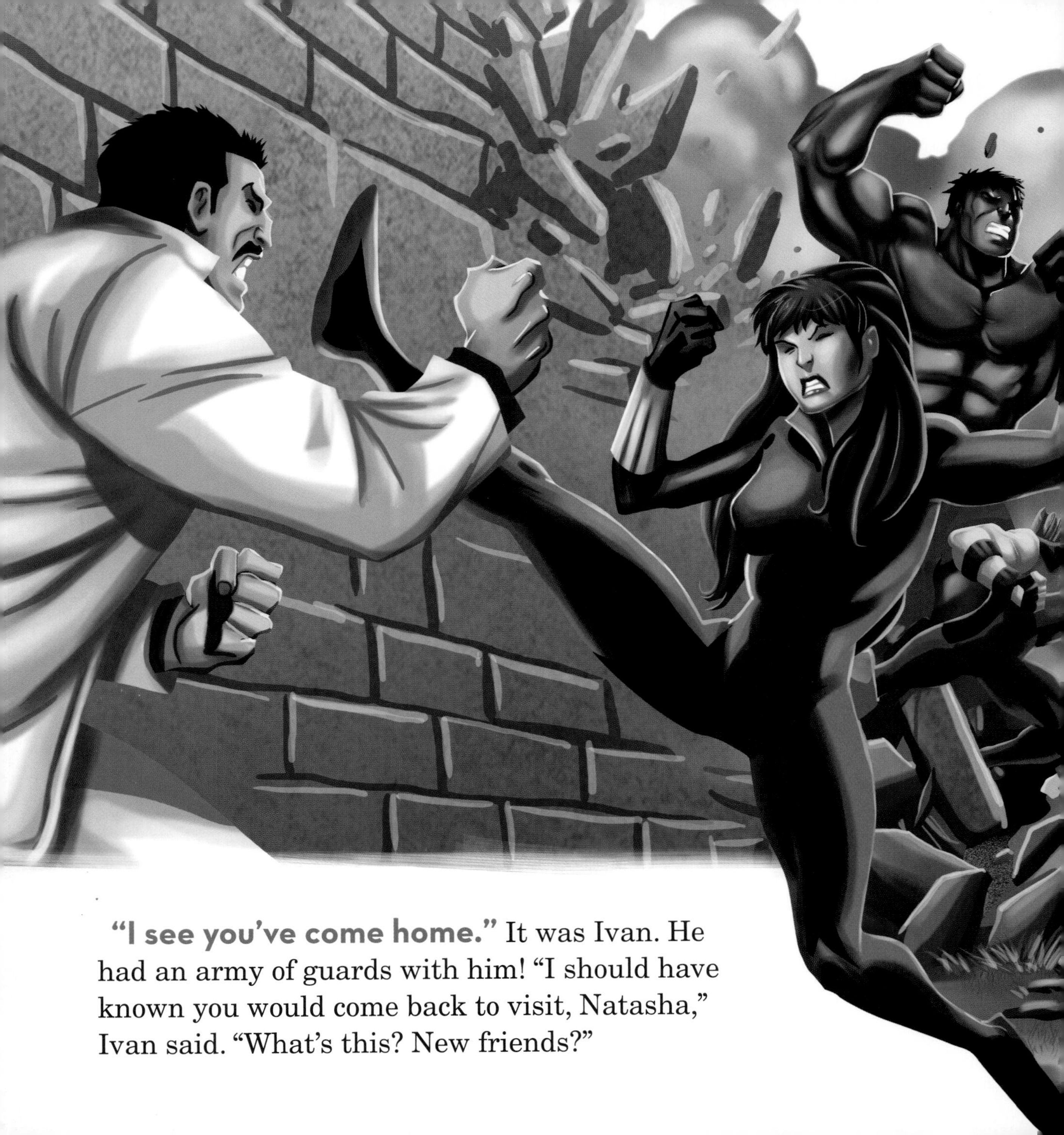

"I see you've come home." It was Ivan. He had an army of guards with him! "I should have known you would come back to visit, Natasha," Ivan said. "What's this? New friends?"

"Where's my brother?" Natasha asked boldly. Ivan only laughed. Angry, she tried to kick Ivan.

"Remember, it was old Ivan who taught you those tricks," Ivan said, as he expertly blocked her attacks.

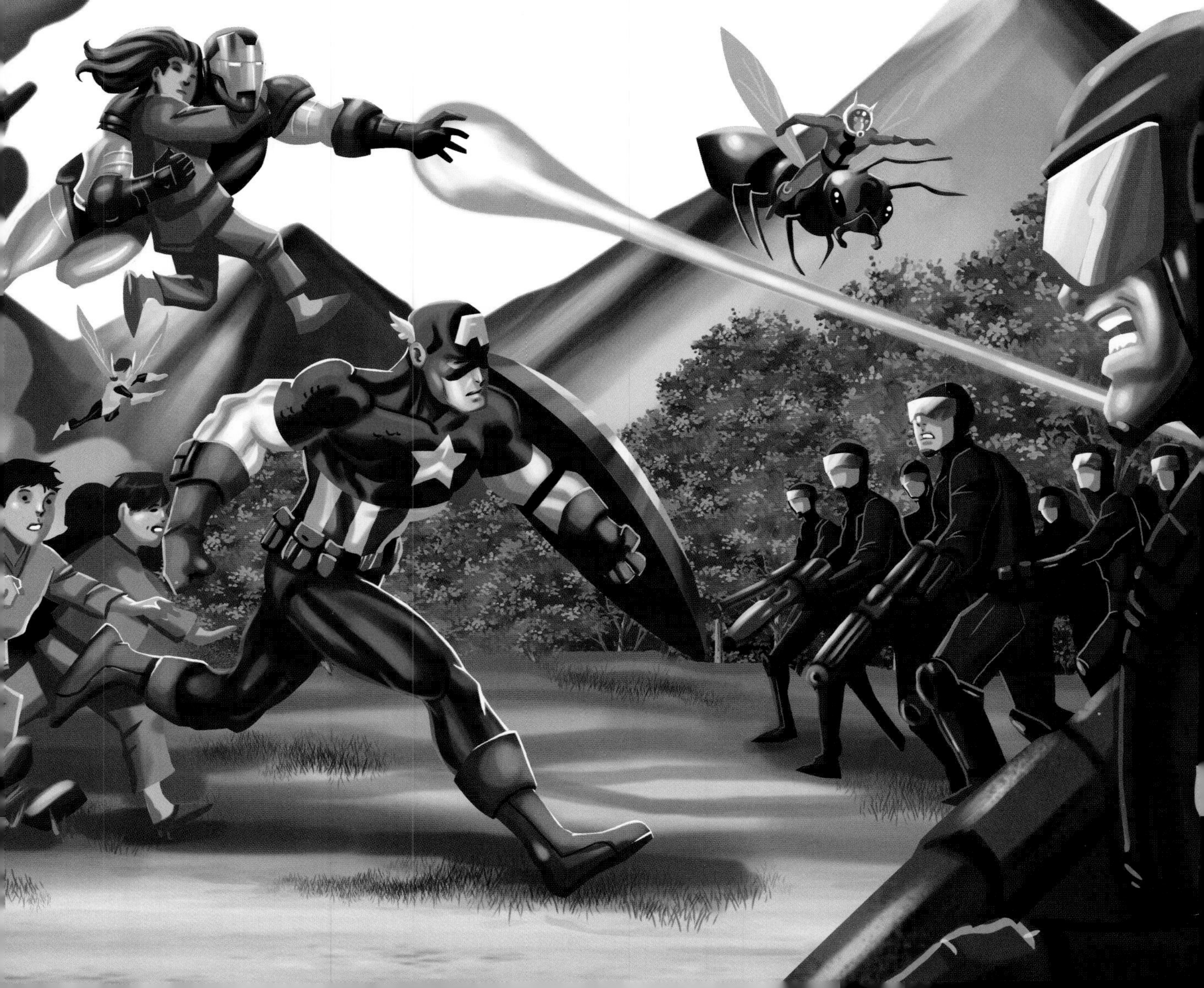

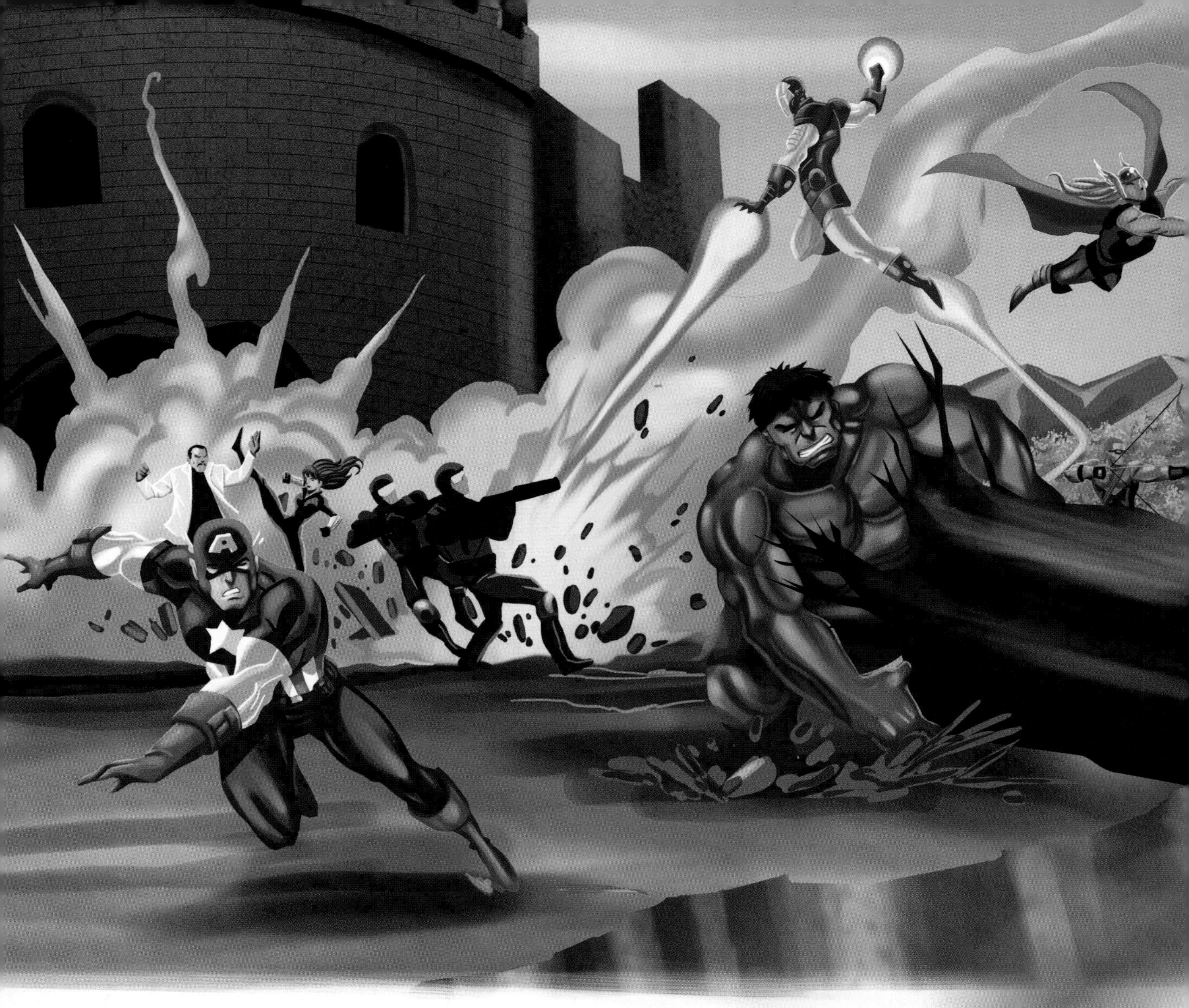

Ivan was much bigger and stronger. But Natasha had speed and cunning on her side. The Avengers freed the children and took on the guards.

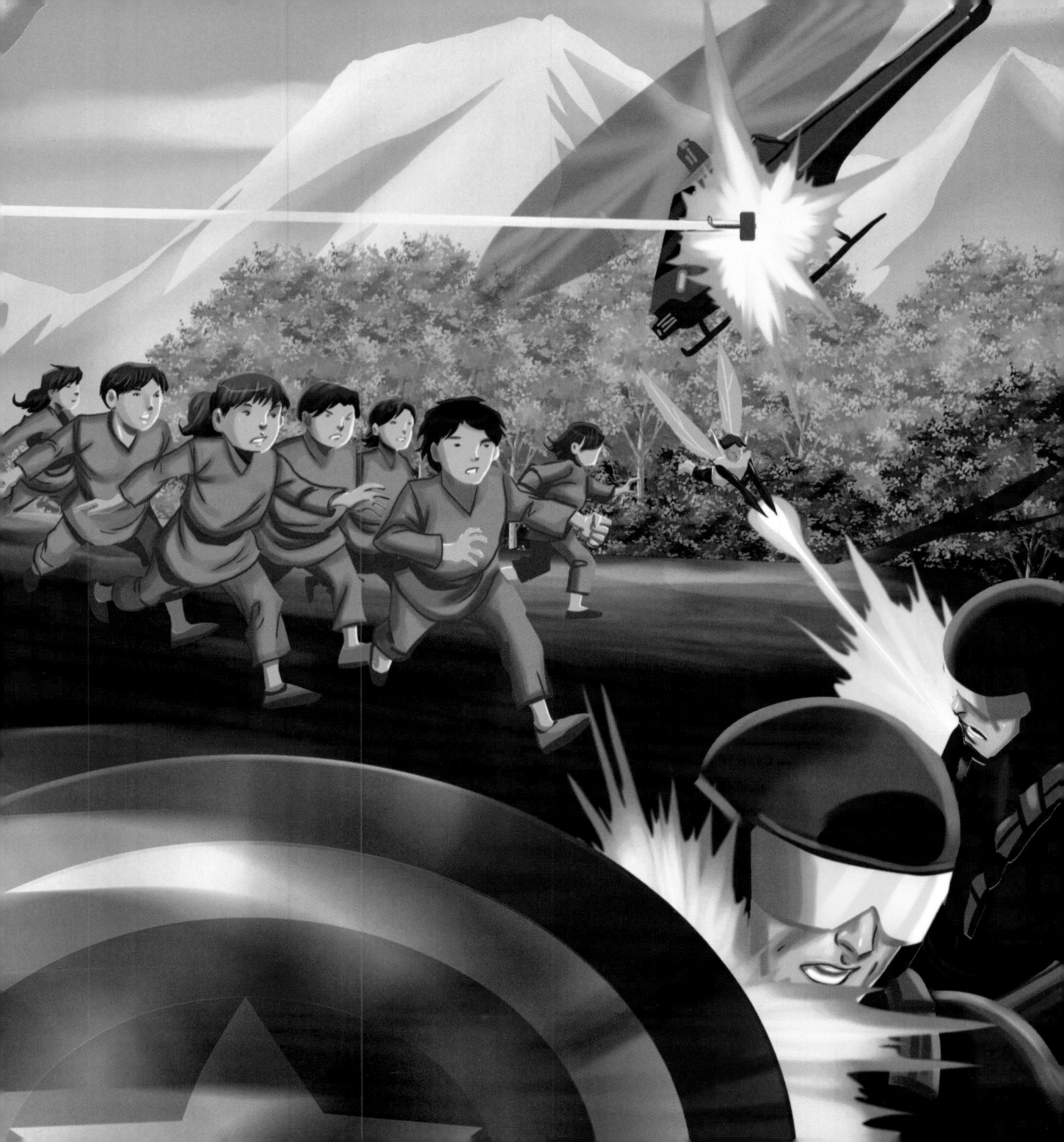

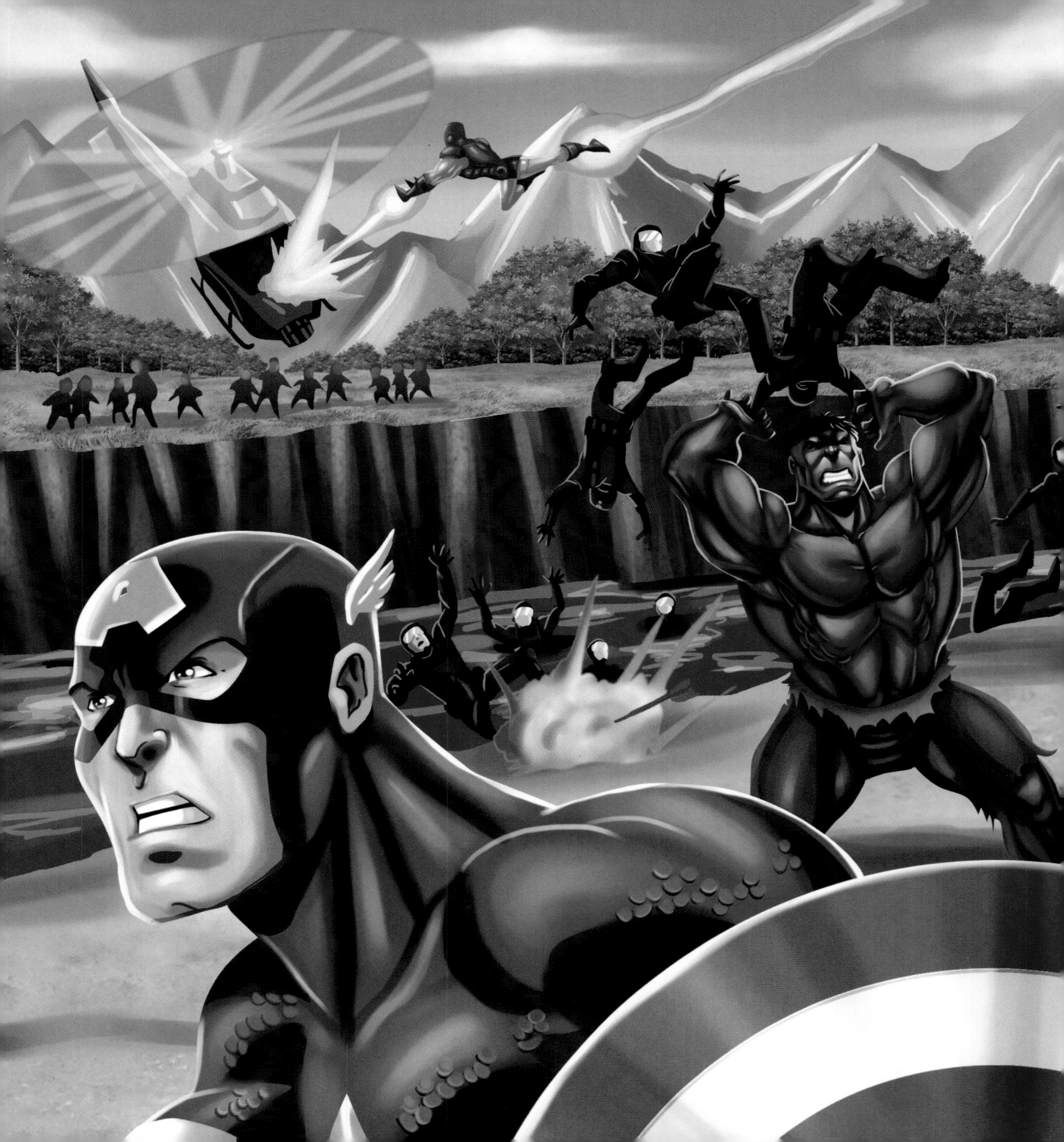

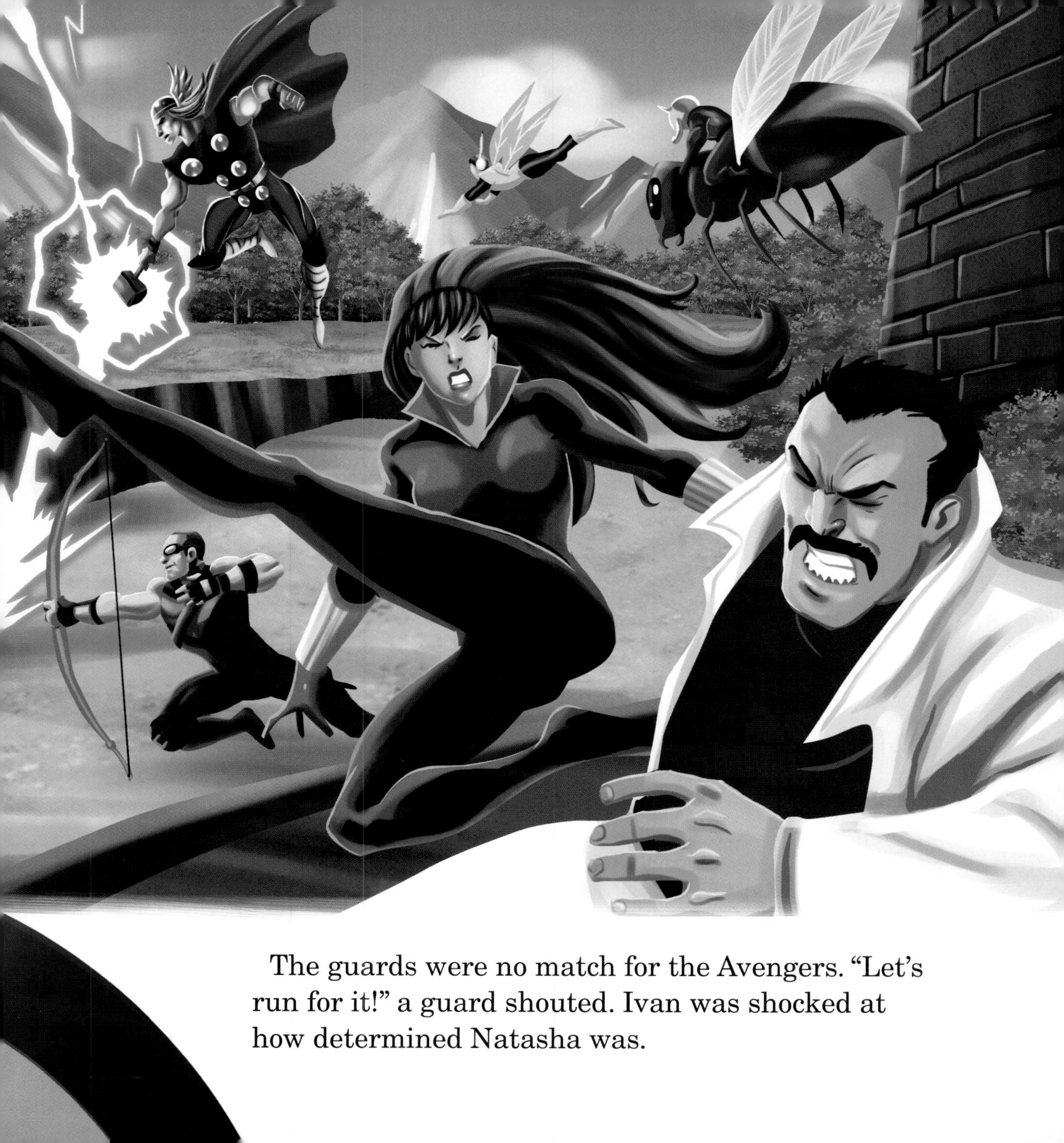

The guards were no match for the Avengers. “Let’s run for it!” a guard shouted. Ivan was shocked at how determined Natasha was.

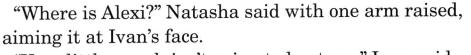

"Where is Alexi?" Natasha said with one arm raised, aiming it at Ivan's face.

"Your little punch isn't going to hurt me," Ivan said, laughing arrogantly.

"Maybe not, but I bet this will," Natasha fired a powerful electric blast from her metal bracelet.

"What was that?" Ivan cried.

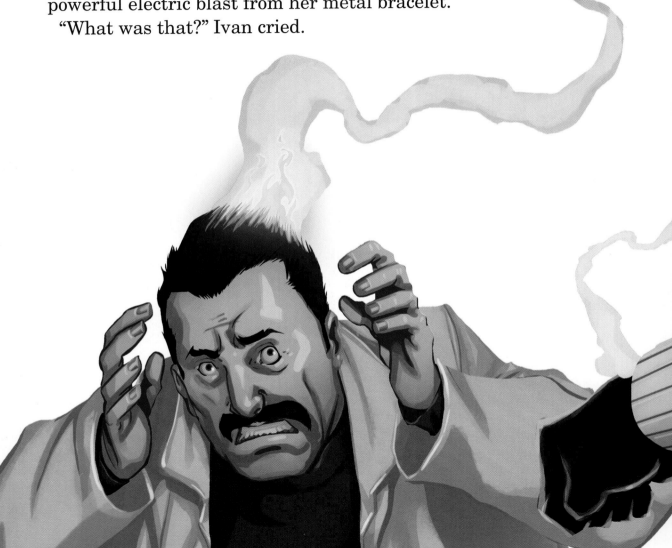

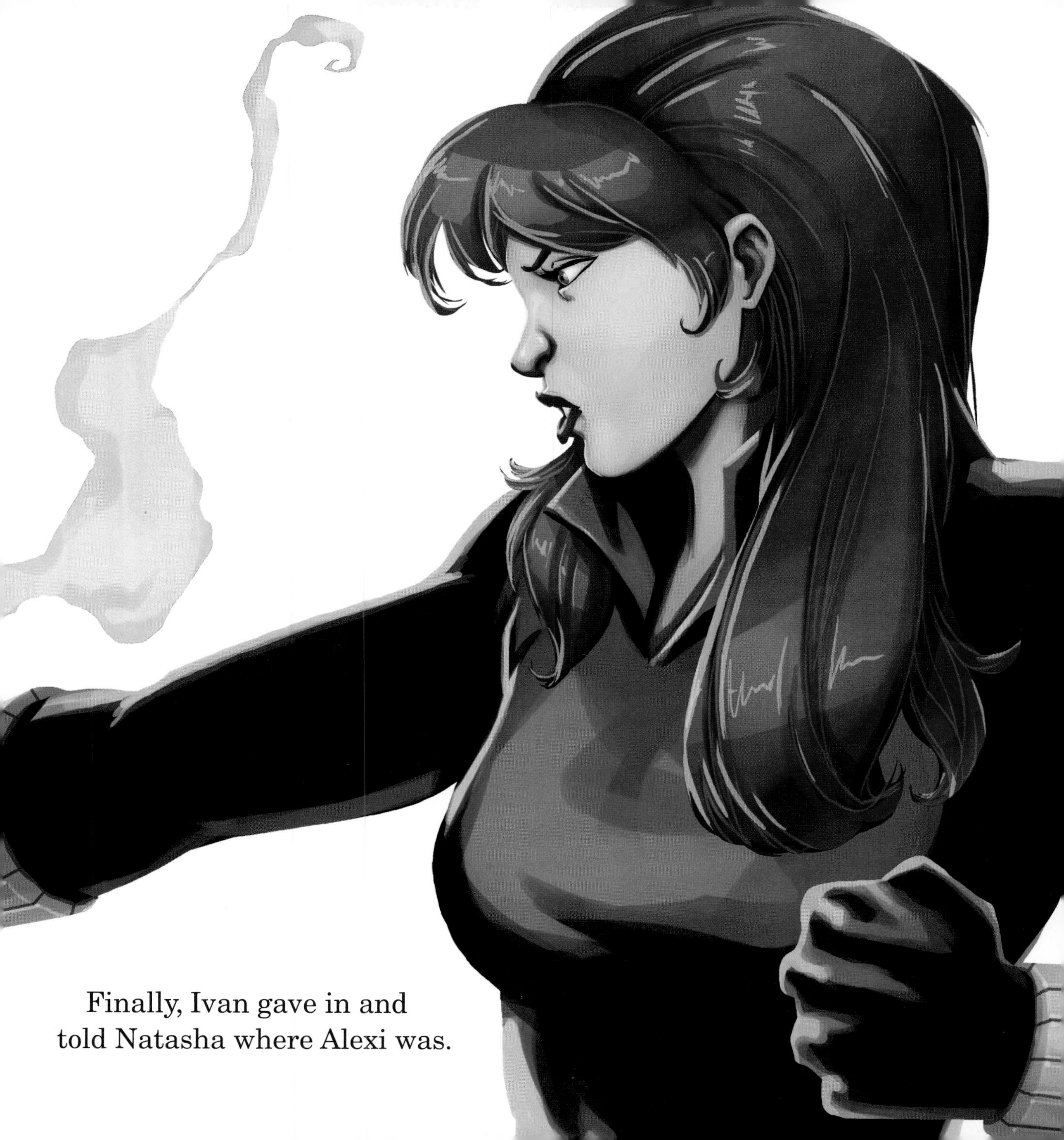

Finally, Ivan gave in and
told Natasha where Alexi was.

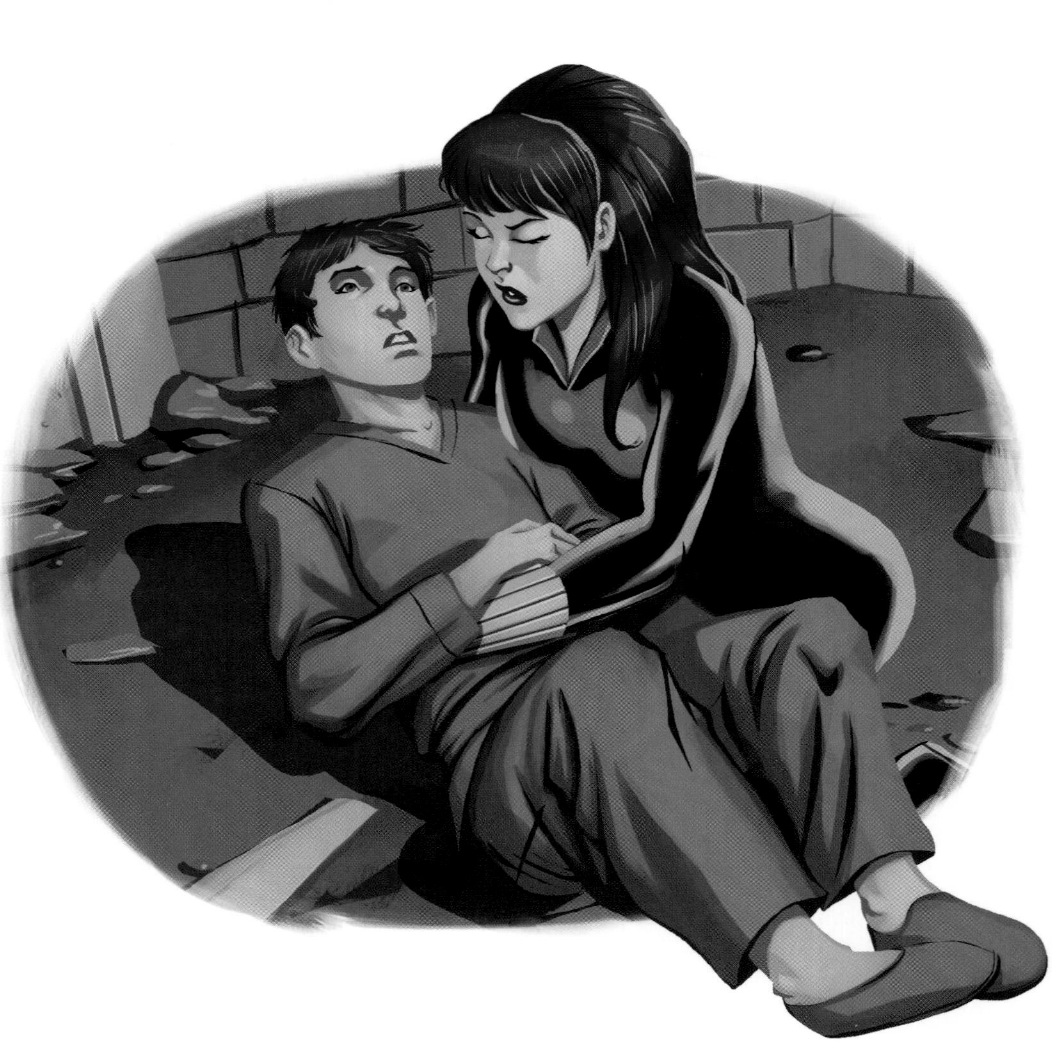

Natasha rushed to where Alexi was locked up. But his eyes were closed, and he looked weak. Am I too late? Natasha thought. **Does he still know who I am?**

"Alexi, are you okay?" Natasha asked. He opened his eyes but did not say anything. Natasha felt her stomach twist.

"What. . . ?" Alexi said faintly.

"What are you doing here? I thought Ivan got rid of you... Natasha..." Alexi said, after he finally got enough energy.

"You're okay!" Natasha shouted with joy and hugged her little brother.

"How did you save me?" Alexi asked, still confused.

"Family always takes care of each other," Natasha answered.

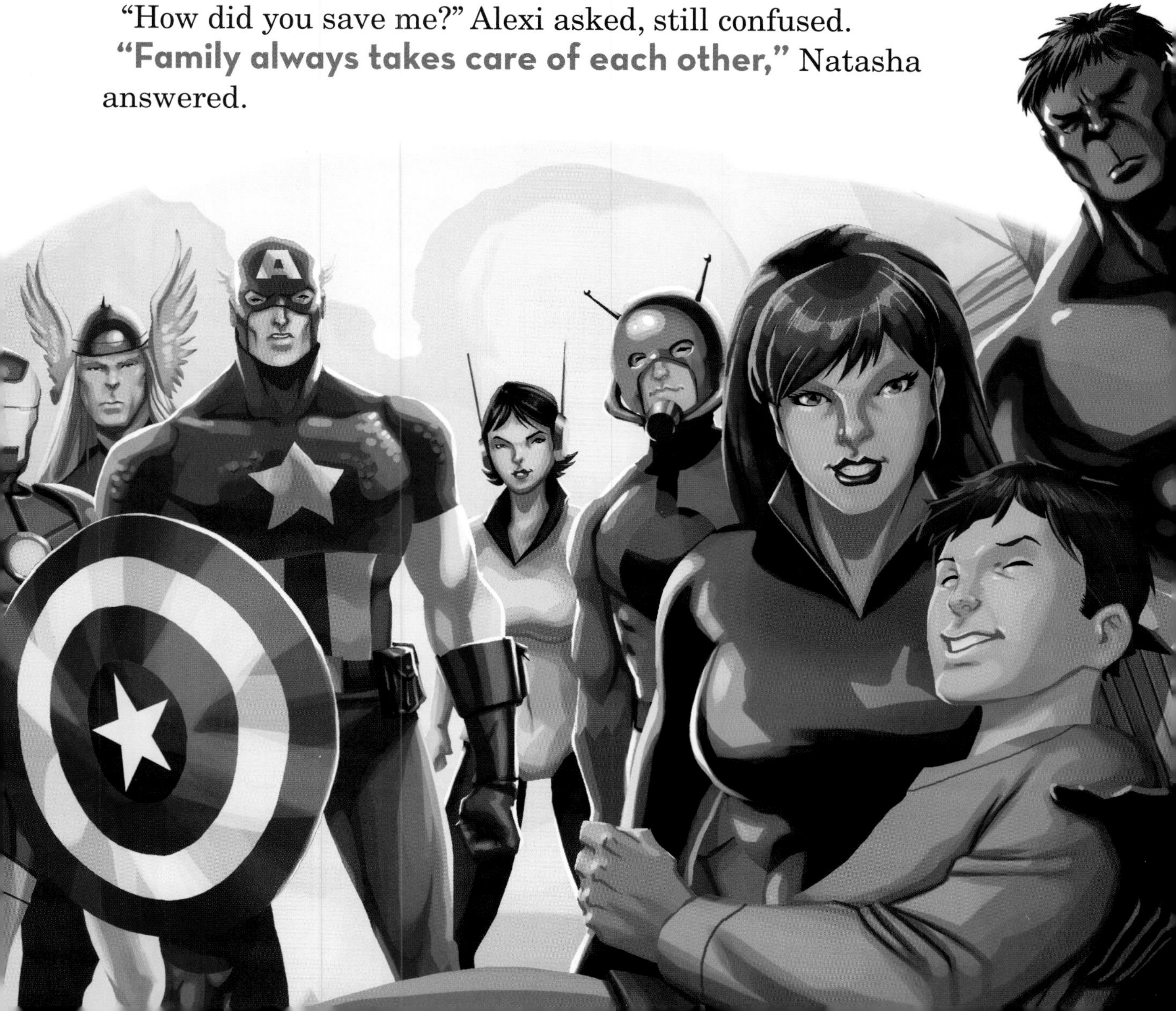

Nick Fury looked impressed with what Natasha had done to protect her little brother.

"I would like you to join Earth's mightiest team of Super Heroes, **the Avengers.** What do you say, Natasha?" Fury asked.

"Count me in! You can call me the **Black Widow,**" Natasha said with a smile.